The Adventures of Munford

THE AMERICAN REVOLUTION

by Jamie Aramini

ILLUSTRATED BY EMILY LEFFERTS

The Adventures of Munford
THE AMERICAN REVOLUTION

Written by Jamie Aramini
Illustrated by Emily Lefferts
Munford character and concepts created by George Wiggers

First Edition

Library of Congress Control Number: 2010925577
ISBN: 978-1-931397-67-4
Published in the U.S.A. by Geography Matters, Inc.®
800-426-4650
www.geomatters.com

Printed in the United States of America

DEDICATION

For Joey and James

ACKNOWLEDGEMENTS

Thanks to Josh and Cindy Wiggers for trusting me with your dream of Munford. I am honored to have the privilege to write this book.

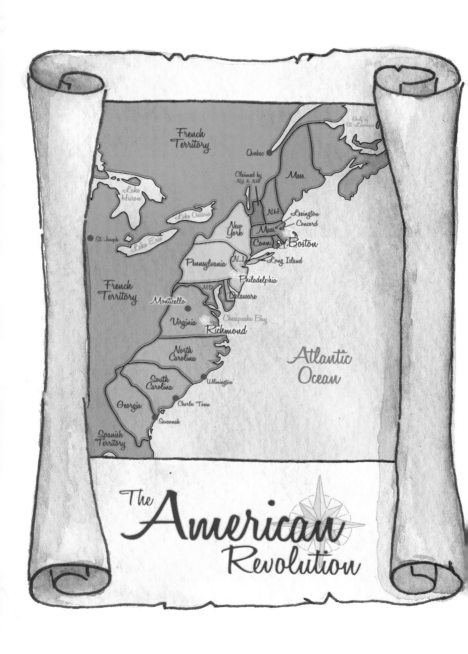

The American Revolution

Table of Contents

Chapter One: MY ARRIVAL IN THE COLONIES 7

Chapter Two: SAMUEL ADAMS 17

Chapter Three: BOSTON TEA PARTY 27

Chapter Four: THE GOVERNOR 35

Chapter Five: THE INTOLERABLE ACTS 43

Chapter Six: FIRST CONTINENTAL CONGRESS 51

Chapter Seven: PAUL REVERE 63

Chapter Eight: A MIDNIGHT RIDE 73

Chapter Nine: LEXINGTON AND CONCORD 83

Chapter Ten: THOMAS JEFFERSON 91

Chapter Eleven: SECOND CONTINENTAL CONGRESS ... 99

Chapter Twelve: THOMAS PAINE 109

Chapter Thirteen: DECLARATION OF INDEPENDENCE .. 115

Chapter Fourteen: VALLEY FORGE 125

Epilogue: A NOTE FROM GRANDPA GILBERT 133

The American Revolution: FASCINATING FACTS 137

Author's Note: SHARING THE VISION OF MUNFORD 139

Chapter One
MY ARRIVAL IN THE COLONIES

KERPLUNK! I landed with a splash in the middle of a mud puddle. Dozens of others fell around me. Oh, boy! This puddle was filling up, and fast.

The water was rising towards the top of the hole it was in. Drip, drop, drip, the rain kept falling down. Closer and closer to the edge we went.

Whooooaaa...the puddle spilled over the top. I was now floating down a street in a rush. What street was it? I didn't know for sure. I had just been in a cloud—What was that? Why, yes, I was in a cloud. Actually, I am in them quite often. You see, I'm a water molecule. My name is Munford. I am two parts hydrogen and one part oxygen. I can be rain, sleet, snow, or fog. I'm not just your average water molecule, either. I'm an adventurer!

Perhaps you've been with me before. Or is this your first adventure? I've been on so many, it is hard to keep track. The great thing about being a water molecule is that I never get old. I simply get recycled again and again and again and—well, you get the idea.

Just a few days ago I was in the ocean. I was there a while, until the sun heated me up. Then, I evaporated. Evaporate is a fancy word that means I turned into a gas. I floated high into the sky where I joined up with other water molecules as I traveled. Together, we formed a cloud.

The cloud slowly filled up with more water. Then I fell down, down, down...splashed into the middle of the puddle. . . and met you! You just never know what will happen when you are a water molecule. This process of turning from liquid to gas and back again is called the water cycle.

The water cycle is how I keep from getting old. It is also how I get from one place to another. The next time you see a rain drop falling on your window, or a drop of dew on the grass, look closely. I might be in there with a thousand others like me. We molecules are very, very tiny—but we sure do get around! Think of all the places the water drop might have been. Think of all the people it might have seen. It sure does make a rainy day a little more fun that way.

It is cool to be a water molecule. I get to travel all over the world and see lots of things in history. As I floated along, I looked for clues as to my location. The streets were made of cobblestones, which are large round stones often used to pave city streets. So, I was in a city rather than the country. The buildings looked like those of a city I had visited before. What was the name of that place? Let me think…Rome, Paris, London…This must be London!

Wait one minute. I had caught a glimpse of the ocean as I was falling from the cloud. This meant I was somewhere along a coast. A coast is the part of the land that meets up with the the ocean.

Does it matter that I was near the coast? Of course, because London is a landlocked town. There

would be no ocean nearby. If I wasn't in London, then where? I slowed to a stop in front of a building with wide steps.

A sign reading "Boston Tavern" hung above the door. So that was it! I was in Boston, Massachusetts. It was my first time here. I had heard of Boston a few weeks ago while I was in London. Boston (and the rest of the American colonies) were the talk of the town over there.

What's a colony? It is a settlement. The colonies in this story are in North America. These thirteen colonies were ruled by Britain's King George III. He had the help of Parliament in running the country.

It is all a little confusing. I hoped it would make more sense now that I was in Boston. A whole ocean (the Atlantic) lies between Britain and the colonies. It took weeks for news to travel from one place to another. So, it was obvious that North America was the best place to learn about the colonies.

I wasn't sure what all the fuss was about, to be honest. I had heard some of the British talk about family and friends who now lived in the colonies. Others weren't so nice. They talked about the Stamp Act and those "rebellious" Americans.

I didn't know why the colonists hated the tax so much. It was a small tax, but the issue wasn't really the tax. The people were upset about their rights. They didn't think Parliament had the right to do that.

It was now 1773. I was confused about it all, so it was quite lucky I had landed in Boston. When you don't know what is going on, go straight to the source. At least, that is what I always say.

I didn't have much longer to think about it.

Adventure always has a way of finding me—if I don't find it first, that is. A fat orange cat sauntered over to the spot where I had stopped. It let out a loud "meow." Oh, dear! It leaned down and peered into the muddy water.

Aahhh! The cat was licking up the water. If I wasn't careful, it was going to get me, too. There are few things worse to a water molecule than getting stuck inside an animal. The cat licked me up, but I managed to stay on his lip. I wasn't going to be anyone's supper tonight. It went into Boston Tavern and I held on for the ride. "Hey there, old fella," the barkeeper said. He reached down and rubbed the cat's face. He wiped me onto his hand in the process. "Head to the back an' the missus will warm you some milk."

The furry creature trotted off to the back of the tavern while the man wiped his hand on a rag. Then he started refilling a customer's mug. I dropped from his hand and grabbed onto the side of the mug. I looked around from my new spot. The tavern was quite empty, I noticed. Only this lone man sat on a barstool.

"Have you heard the news?" the man asked in the direction of the barkeeper.

"I don't know what you are talking about," he said.

"Ah," said the man. "Can ye get me a cup of coffee then?"

Behind the counter, the barkeeper didn't move to make any coffee. "Alright, what is it, sir?" It seemed pretty obvious to me. The man just wanted some coffee.

"We will meet tonight. Sam thinks it is time to take action. We must do something about that blasted tea. He says we won't let it in the harbor. It will be coffee or nothing for those loyal to the cause."

Hmm…it seemed the man's coffee order had just been some kind of secret code.

"Tell Mr. Adams he can count me in. It was bad enough when King George thought he could profit from our tea with that ridiculous tax. And now to limit who can sell it! What will it be next, I ask? They'll be telling me what ale I can serve, that's what. I won't stand by and—" He stopped talking as two men in red coats came in and took a seat. I knew from the red that they were British soldiers.

The man took one last drink from his mug, catching me up with it. He wiped his mouth with the back of his hand. I held onto a ring he wore as he tossed some change onto the counter and headed outside with a nod. "I'll let 'em know you're coming, then." With that, we headed out the door and into the street.

Chapter Two

SAMUEL ADAMS

I didn't know the name of the man I traveled with and I didn't like that one bit. I always make it a habit to learn a man's name. Whoever he was, he stayed busy all day, going from business to business. Everywhere we went, the message was the same. Something had to be done about the tea. A man named Sam Adams had sent the message.

As we left each new business, the messenger marked a list with a stubby piece of chalk. I couldn't get a clear view because of the setting sun, but it must have been a list with the names of those people to contact. I began to feel a buzz of excitement. What were they going to do about the tea? I didn't have any idea. I did have a feeling that I had found what I was looking for. This felt like my next adventure.

The sun had dipped out of the sky by the time we reached the last stop of the night. A small sign with the name Adams was posted at the gate. This must be where the mysterious Samuel Adams lived. I hoped I would get to see him.

The man didn't go to the door like he had at the other places. He knocked on a darkened side window, making a sharp rap-rap-rap noise. The window opened just a small bit and the man pulled the list from his pocket. He reached toward the window...

Oh no! He was going to throw it inside, wasn't he? It looked like I might not meet Mr. Adams after all. This was my only chance, so I leaped onto the paper just in the nick of time. He tossed it into the window. The paper, with me hanging on, fluttered to the wooden floor. I heard the window close with a soft thump. Someone pulled the curtains shut. The room was dark. Several minutes of silence went by.

All I could hear was the tick-tick-tick of the clock and the crackle of a fireplace in another room.

The paper was soon picked up and me with it. We were carried into another room where a crackling fire lit up the space. Now I could see who carried me. It was an older gentleman, dressed in the fashion of other middle class Bostonians. The wrinkles around his eyes showed a look of concern as he unfolded the list.

Another man stepped up beside him, and they read over the list by the light of the fire. "Do you think it will be enough, Samuel?"

"Hmm. . . around eighty men. It should be enough, John."

"I suppose you're right. I think the message will be clear."

Samuel nodded. "It will be. We have waited around long enough. For once, the people of Boston are in agreement. Parliament cannot tax our tea and then tell us from whom to buy it."

"Aye," said John. "You're a good man, Sam.

You have rallied the people to our cause. Are you sure you want to go through with this? It will change everything, I think."

"It's a risk I'm willing to take."

A maid entered the room, startling both of the men. "I'm so sorry, Mr. Adams. I didn't know you were still meeting."

Mr. Adams nodded. "No worries, Eliza. Mr. Hancock was just leaving." He tossed the list into the blazing fire and the paper was quickly consumed by the flames. The heat turned me into vapor in an instant. The hot air carried me up the chimney and out into the night air.

The streets of Boston were mostly quiet. I thought about my brief time with Sam Adams and the man named John Hancock. Who were they? Why was he calling so many men to his meeting?

I found myself joining up with other water molecules floating above the town of Boston. We began to form a cloud, but it was the next evening before our little cloud was full enough to precipitate. (It all sounds familiar, doesn't it? As a water molecule, we tend to do the same things over and over. Now you can understand why it is called the water cycle.)

I became part of a snowflake slowly floating towards the streets of Boston. Thousands of other snowflakes swirled around me. It was a beautiful sight to see each one glistening in the moonlight.

I landed on a man's wool coat as he walked the streets of Boston. The snow went crunch crunch under his feet. He went to a darkened building and entered through a side door. As he descended a flight of stairs, I could hear voices, which grew louder the farther we went. I soon found myself in a room full of men talking and shouting in angry voices.

There was Samuel Adams! He was standing at the front of the room, doing his best to talk over the voices of the other men. "The new Tea Act gives the East India Company control over who can sell tea in the colonies. It is an outrage! Parliament should have no say over who can sell to the colonies. For now it is tea, but soon they will control everything we do. We must put a stop to it."

"Here! Here!" the men cried out.

Another man, whom I remembered as John Hancock, said, "Three ships are waiting in Boston Harbor to unload their tea. We've placed guards to make sure the tea stays on board, but we must make a decision tonight."

"Send it back to the motherland," someone said.

A short gentleman who wore small round spectacles stood to his feet. He said in a shaking

voice, "N-n-n-no, it can't b-b-be done. The t-t-teeaa agents re-f-f-fuse."

"There you have it, gentlemen. The tea must be destroyed."

"I don't understand it. Why can't we just let them unload the tea, but no one buy any of it?" one of the men asked.

"Yes. What about that?" another said.

"Letting them unload the tea won't do anything. It will still be taxed. If we do it our way, we will send a clear message that we will not be enslaved by Parliament! They know nothing about us. We will stand up for liberty!" The men rose to their feet and cheered.

"Hurrah for the Sons of Liberty! Hurrah!" The Sons of Liberty was a term I had heard before. I'm not sure who started it, but it was the name given to the men who disagreed with British rule.

"The tea must be destroyed," said Samuel.

"Boston Harbor a teapot tonight!" the men cried in unison. Samuel's smooth words had inspired them. He had a way of showing others what was wrong, and he also had good ideas about what to do to fix it.

The decision was made, and the men filtered out into the street. I rode out on the man's shoulder, wondering where we would go next. What had they meant when they called the harbor a teapot? It all seemed a little strange if you asked me. I decided I would stick around to find out. I had hoped to leave with Samuel Adams. Since I didn't get a chance, I stayed with the man I had come in with.

Chapter Three
BOSTON TEA PARTY

The cold December air left me frozen solid. I stayed with the man as he went home. He gathered some supplies into a sack, but I could hardly tell what they were because of the darkness.

It was several hours later when we arrived at another dark building. We entered after the man mumbled some sort of password about the Sons of Liberty. We were not the first to arrive, and I knew some of the men who were there. I remembered them from my time with the messenger. They were all different kinds of people. They were all different ages, too. As each one came in, he emptied a sack onto the floor.

All the men, squeezed together in the small space, made the room warm up. As more men came in, the warmer and warmer it got. Soon, their body heat had warmed the room so much that I was a liquid again. I dripped into a small tin can that one of the men carried. What had I gotten myself into now? I found myself surrounded by a dark, gooey substance.

"Give me some of that," one of the men said. The can, with me in it, was promptly handed over.

The man dipped his thumb into the can and smeared the substance across his face, taking me with it. Face paint! I had fallen into a tin of paint. I now found myself painted right onto the man's nose. It was a good vantage point, I decided, because I could clearly see everything that was going on.

I was glad I could see. Quite a change had occurred, and the men no longer wore their regular clothes. Everyone had also used the tin can with the paint. Standing before me was no longer a ragtag group of merchants, fishmongers, and teenage boys. Instead, I saw a group of American natives, complete with feathered headdresses. No one would know them now.

"For Boston!" one of the men said.

"For liberty!" said another.

With that, they headed out the door. Their moccasins muffled the sound of their footsteps. What would people think about them if they were seen? That was unlikely though, because most of the city was sound asleep in their beds. They had no idea what was going to happen. Neither did I.

The group traveled quietly along the streets of Boston. More and more men joined us as we went. All were in native dress and I noticed that each of them carried a hatchet. What were those for? I hoped I wouldn't have to see them put to use.

Snow continued to fall from the sky. The dock was eerily quiet as the men walked the wooden planks. I noticed many different ships and boats along the dock. Their shapes cast strange shadows in the moonlight. I could hear the ocean waves softly hitting the sides of the boats.

"Let's split up," said one of the men. "We'll take the Dartmouth. You all take the other two." The group separated, and the man I was with headed towards a large ship. The word Dartmouth was painted on the side. Once on board, we quickly went down to the cargo hold. "Find the crates marked tea," the leader said. I didn't know who he was—it was too hard to tell through the disguise.

There were many other goods on board besides tea. I scanned the crates. Sugar…Flour… Spice…Tea! There were crates upon crates with that label.

"Just the tea, men," said the leader of the group. "Nothing else is to be damaged. We want them to know that it is the tea we are after."

The men lugged the huge crates up onto deck one at a time. The crates looked so plain. There had been so much talk about the tea, I guess I thought it would look scarier. I thought it would seem like danger. It was hard to understand what the problem was, because the tea by itself seemed innocent.

Out came the hatchets, and the men started tearing into the wood. Hack! Hack! Hack! The crates splintered with the force of each blow.

"Overboard!" They shoved the tea over the siderail. Splash! The tea landed in the water. "This will show them we mean business. Our voice must be heard in Parliament!"

"What a waste," one young man said.

"A small price to pay for our liberties," replied one of the older gentlemen.

"Can't we just take a wee bit home?" someone asked. The scent of dried tea leaves was getting stronger and stronger.

"I want none of the stuff if it comes from the East India Company. I'll drink coffee the rest of my life if I have to."

"You're right about that! No one takes any home. Every last drop must go into the harbor tonight!" someone shouted.

I watched and listened. I was glad I had gotten stuck in the gooey paint because I didn't want to get thrown overboard with the tea. Accidents do happen, you know.

I kept a lookout for any strange activity. I didn't want to get caught. I do like adventure, but I do try to stay out of trouble! It seemed to me that these weren't the kind of men who liked to get into trouble either. They had good lives and happy families. Why were they willing to throw it away over the tea? If they got caught, it would mean prison for sure.

The only thing I could figure is that they did it to stay happy. They wanted to be sure that they had freedoms, and they wanted their kids to have freedoms, too. They didn't want the government running everything. It was even worse since they were given no say in how things went.

Hack! Hack! Hack! The men worked late into the night. Just before the sun began to peek above the horizon, this strange native tribe left Boston Harbor. Still painted onto a face, I left with them.

I had hoped to stick on board the Dartmouth a little longer so that I could see the reaction of the deck hands when they came aboard. The Sons of Liberty left the ship in tip-top shape. They even swept the bits of splintered wood into the ocean. The only sign that anyone had been there would be the missing tea and the tinted water swirling below.

Chapter Four
THE GOVERNOR

I went home stuck to the same face where I had been painted. We left the group and turned onto a side street. The man entered what I thought was his home through the back door, and then he wasted no time. His feathers and native clothes were tossed into the fireplace. The flames destroyed them quickly.

The man went through a side door where a woman and small child slept on a narrow bed. He kissed them both on their foreheads. I wondered if they knew where he had been. Now in regular clothes, he washed his face and sat down to rest. I was still on his face, so I waited with him, pondering my next move.

It seemed like forever before something happened. I heard the tinkle tinkle of a bell in the next room. The man jumped from his chair.

"I'll be right out," he shouted. We headed into the front room, which was actually a butcher shop. It was early morning and a customer had already arrived. The woman was waiting with an empty basket.

"I'm here to pick up the order for the Governor's mansion," she said.

"Yes, Sally, I believe I have it around here somewhere..." He started sorting through some packages. "How are things at the mansion?"

"Ah, good as can be expected, I guess." She sighed. "The governor will be fit to be tied once he wakes up and hears the news."

The butcher stopped what he was doing. "The news?"

Sally smiled. "I hear ol' Sam Adams had himself quite the tea party in Boston Harbor last night."

The butcher found the packages. "Oh...Sam Adams, you say? I heard it was a tribe of rogue natives."

"What good would it do the natives to destroy the tea? It seems they'd be better off to steal it," she said.

"You've got a point there. Maybe old Sam finally lost his patience."

"Maybe," said Sally. "We're all fed up with it, I guess. I just wonder who Sam got to help him."

"Who knows?" said the butcher. "Who knows…"

"By the way, sir, you appear to have a bit of something smeared below your left eye," Sally pointed out.

"I wonder where that could have come from…" he said, wiping off the paint and me with it. I grabbed onto one of the packages to keep from falling to the ground. "Well, have a good day, Miss." He handed her the packages to go in her basket.

"And the same to you, kind sir," said Sally.

Sally left the butcher shop with me tucked safely in her basket. She stopped at several other merchants as the morning progressed. She even bought some fresh vegetables to go with the butcher's meat.

I soon found myself in the kitchen at the Governor's mansion. Sally unloaded her purchases onto a wooden tabletop and set about preparing breakfast. I had no choice but to go along for the ride. I had a nice tour of the kitchen as I was transferred from place to place. Eventually, I ended up with other water molecules in a kettle over a hot fire. We slowly heated up, up, up until the whole kettle reached the boiling point. Do you know what that is? The boiling point is the temperature when water begins to boil, which greatly speeds up the process of evaporation.

Water boils at around two hundred and twelve degrees Fahrenheit.

The kettle was removed from the fire and I soon found myself swimming around in none other than a pot of tea. I found it quite ironic, keeping in mind what I had done last night. A butler took me directly to what I assumed was the Governor's office. Thomas Hutchinson was the governor of Massachusetts, chosen by King George. It was his job to oversee the colony. One part of his job was to make sure that imported goods were safely unloaded and properly taxed. I wondered how he would react when he heard the news.

The Governor sat at his desk reviewing some papers. He looked up as the door opened. "Oh, I see you've brought breakfast. How delightful. My stomach was just starting to growl."

The butler placed the tray on the table. "Sir," he said as he poured tea, and me, from the kettle into a cup, "a messenger has brought some dismal news from Boston Harbor."

The Governor sighed. "What is it now?"

"I'm afraid there was an episode, sir, with the tea."

"You mean the tea aboard the Dartmouth?" The Governor picked up his tea cup and took a small sip. I managed to avoid going down the hatch, as they say.

"Yes, sir, and two other ships. It seems that some of the tea has gone missing."

"Missing? How much?"

"Well..." the butler hesitated. "All of it, sir—342 crates, according to the inventory log."

Hutchinson slammed down his tea cup, sloshing me out of the side and onto the tray. "Please tell me how that much tea can just go missing! Surely someone would have seen it being hauled down the streets of Boston! These blasted colonists don't have a warehouse big enough to hide that much tea."

The butler backed towards the door. "The thing is, they've found the tea. It's...it's...in the harbor. They dumped it. All of it."

The Governor let out a disgusted grunt. "Take this breakfast away. I'm afraid I've lost my appetite.

I want names. I want to know who did this. I already
know one name you can put at the top of the list:
Samuel Adams."

The butler gathered up the breakfast, and me
with it, and headed out. "Yes, sir."

"And that other meddlesome man, John
Hancock. I know they are at the bottom of this!"

Yikes! The Governor was pretty mad. I didn't
blame him. All that tea was gone to waste now, and
there would be a lot of people angry with him for

not putting a stop to it. King George would be really mad. He might even fire the Governor. Maybe it was a good thing that it would take weeks before he found out what happened.

Chapter Three
THE INTOLERABLE ACTS

Things were quiet around Boston during the weeks following the Tea Party. It seemed that they were all waiting to see what would happen. How would the King react? What would change? What would stay the same?

The Governor needed someone to blame for the tea. The problem was who, because his hunch about Samuel Adams could not be confirmed. Governor Hutchinson sent word to Parliament about what had happened to see what they wanted to do.

He didn't receive a response right away. After all, Parliament was all the way in Britain. News had to travel across the Atlantic Ocean by ship. Then a decision had to be made before the news could travel back over the Atlantic and to Boston.

When Parliament's decision finally did arrive, it was worse than what anyone had expected. The home of Samuel Adams was a flurry of activity. I somehow ended up there, carried in by the wind of a sneeze. "This is intolerable!" Samuel shouted. "They cannot do this. It isn't right!"

"Tell us what has happened," said one of the men.

"The Navy has arrived," said Samuel. "They aren't here to protect us loyal British citizens, either."

"What do you mean?" someone else asked.

"They've closed down Boston Harbor and no ships can enter or leave. No supplies for the citizens of Boston! Only for the Governor and his soldiers."

"This is an outrage!"

"Unbelievable!"

The men all had the same feelings. The people of Boston relied on shipments from other colonies and countries. Each shipment contained food and supplies. The people of Boston needed these things to survive

and conduct business. Without a port, Boston could only receive supplies through a narrow strip of land. The other three sides of the city were water.

"Why should all of Boston be punished for our actions? Only a few dumped the tea, only a few should be punished," one said.

I thought he made a good point. Mr. Adams was upset, too. "This is just proof that Britain is no longer worried about us. They don't care about whether or not our children have food to eat tonight. They are only concerned with their silly tax money."

Others asked him, "Aren't you worried? How will we eat?"

To this question, Sam only laughed. "We'll eat just like those who came before us did. We'll live off of the land, if we must! We can fish off the shore and hunt for clams."

Sam spent most of the week with visitors. It felt like all of Boston came to him with their concerns. He did his best to answer their questions and comfort them.

Several days had passed when the strangest thing started to happen. News had spread quickly through the colonies about what was going on in Boston. Many people wanted to show their support. They sent wagonloads of supplies, including corn, wheat, and rice. New York even sent some sheep! All over America, people were worried about Boston and they wanted to help.

Letters came with many of the gifts. Samuel read some of them. "They're afraid," he told John Hancock. "They see what King George is doing to Boston, and wonder what he will do next. Which colony will spark his anger next month or next year?"

John Hancock nodded. "The same thing. He'll do the same thing to any colony that crosses him. What about the new proclamation?"

"All government positions will now be appointed by the King or by the Governor," Sam said. "We are no longer free to choose who serves in the legislature. There will be no hope for us now. Only those who do not question the King will be able to serve in government posts."

"You must call a meeting," John replied. "We should alert the people to this unfairness. Let them decide how to act."

Samuel sighed. "Things are only going to get worse, I'm afraid. I only hope that the public can be stirred to action. I will hold a meeting," he said. "It must be kept secret. The King has also banned public meetings, a law which I'm sure was directed right at us and the rest of the Sons of Liberty!"

Both men fell silent. By choosing to hold a secret meeting, they would be breaking the law. They would be standing up against the King. If caught, the punishment would be severe.

Samuel Adams knew he would have to take the risk of being caught. "The colonies need a new government, a government that will represent them, a government that will look out for the people instead of finding new ways to harm them. We will stand up for what we believe in. It will be a busy week. I will send my messenger with word when the meeting time is set."

I liked being with Mr. Adams. He was always in the middle of the action, even though it was a different kind of action than I was used to. He didn't sail the high seas or climb mountains. He didn't explore new territories or fight big battles. Yet, he was still an adventurer. His life was an adventure of words.

Not all visitors to Mr. Adams were friendly. Some were upset. They came to tell him how angry they were because they felt that the closing of the port and the other laws were his fault. He had, after all, stirred the men to dump the tea into the harbor. He had encouraged those who were loyal to the King to see the colonists' point of view.

Mr. Adams was unmoved by their anger. He had a way of turning their own arguments against them. He was a great debater. "What the King has done is intolerable," he would say. All who came to visit left feeling like they should do whatever it took to free themselves from British rule. Something must be done about the "Intolerable Acts," as they came to be called. This was, of course, the goal of Samuel Adams. This was what he was working towards.

One day Mr. Adams received a message from the colony of Virginia. They wanted to meet with the other colonies to decide whether or not something could be done to protect American settlers from the King's wrath. The message asked for representatives from each of the colonies to meet in Philadelphia for the First Continental Congress. This was just the kind of thing that Mr. Adams had been waiting for.

Chapter Six
FIRST CONTINENTAL CONGRESS

I was starting to feel a little cooped up staying in the home of Samuel Adams. One of the bad things about being a water molecule is that you can't always go just where you want when you want. Some force of nature has to move you along. Even when you do move, it might not be to the exact place you were wanting to go.

Still, I tried to be patient. I knew that soon Mr. Adams would be traveling to Philadelphia as one of the representatives of the Congress, and I certainly didn't want to miss that trip.

When the time came to head out, I was lucky to get packed away in the water canteen. I did not want to get left behind, so it didn't matter that I was crammed so tightly in the dark space with all those other molecules. Eventually, I was sloshed out onto the side of the canteen when Mr. Adams took a drink. I had a much better view point that way!

The trip to Philadelphia took many days. I could tell that Samuel Adams was growing tired because as the trip went on, he seemed to slouch over more and more. He spent most of his time in deep thought. I imagined that he was going over what he would say to the other people at the Congress. Some other delegates also came from Massachusetts.

It was after dark when our carriage arrived in Philadelphia. I couldn't get a good view of the city, but hoped to in the morning. We went to the inn where we would be staying, and Samuel was soon fast asleep.

The next morning he was up with the sunrise. I managed to join him, on his shoulder once again, as we went out into the streets of the city. I was surprised at what I saw!

The sun had just risen, but the streets were already filling up. Philadelphia was bustling with

action. "The largest city in the colonies," I had heard Samuel say. He must have been right, for it seemed to be larger than Boston.

We made our way to a meeting hall, called Carpenter's Hall. It was a plain two story building made of red bricks. It had lots of windows. I wondered how much adventure could go on in this building.

I was starting to get a little bit tired. If you remember, I was in Boston looking for adventure. I wanted some action! The Boston Tea Party was pretty neat. Ever since then, though, it was just talking. Talk, talk, talk. It seemed like that was all these people did. Day in and day out, they talked and argued about what should be done.

Being the great adventurer that I am, all this talking was wearing me out. I was ready for some action! "Let's quit talking and do something"—that is what I would say if I were part of the meeting. I decided to stick around a little while longer, but if things didn't pick up soon, I was going to have to move on. I could hear a new adventure calling my name.

It was already September. The weather was still warm and inside the building, it wasn't any better. The twelve colonies had sent a total of fifty-six representatives. Fifty-six! It made the temperature in the room go up, up, up. It became so warm, in fact, that I evaporated. No longer attached to Samuel Adams, I was free to float around the room. Boy, was I glad!

I will spare you all the details of what went on. It was just more talking and more arguing. They talked about the "Intolerable Acts" and what should be done about them. They talked about how to best defend the freedom of the colonies.

Some of the men believed that the colonies should form a type of government that would be separate from the King and would have to approve whatever measures the King took. Some of the men didn't want to accept any of the King's measures. Others wanted to reconcile with the King and stay completely under British authority.

All those opinions made it hard to come to any decisions. This went on for days and days and days. I just kept floating around the building, waiting for something to happen and wondering how long it would take.

Just when I was starting to get fed up, the strangest thing happened. I was looking out the window of Carpenter's Hall. One of the delegates was droning on about the need to stay loyal to Britain. It seemed like we had heard it all before at this point. Anyway, I was just gazing out the window in a daze.

Suddenly, I heard the clickety-clickety-clack of a galloping horse. A horse and rider came speeding up towards the door of the hall. Who could this be? What could he want? Whatever it was, it looked like adventure to me!

The man came into the room with a document rolled up under his arm. The room fell quiet and the leader of the Congress, a man named Peyton Randolph, stood up. "My goodness, man, what is it?"

The man removed his hat. It was then that I knew he was Paul Revere, although I didn't know much about him. He was from Boston, and I had seen him at a few meetings of the Sons of Liberty.

"I've come as fast as I could. I thought that the members of the First Continental Congress needed to hear this. It is a document written and adopted by the leaders of Suffolk County."

I knew Suffolk County was in Masschusetts and included the city of Boston. I wondered what it said. What could have been so important that this man came all that way?

"Well, then," said Mr. Randolph, "I guess if

you've come all that way, the Congress will hear what you have to say."

"Hear, hear," said the men.

Paul unrolled the papers and began to read. It was a lot to take in, but I managed to catch bits and pieces. The men of Suffolk County believed that the Intolerable Acts were nothing more than a way to make slaves of the Americans. They believed that anyone hired by the King to work in the colonies should resign. If they didn't, the colonists should force them from their posts. How would they do that, I wondered?

Almost as if he knew what I was thinking, Paul said, "This will be done by a town militia." Oh, my. A town militia meant that the citizens would get together and form their own small armies. I knew that the King wouldn't like that one bit!

The Suffolk Resolves, as the document was called, seemed to inspire the Congress. They cheered as it was being read, although I did notice a few who remained quiet. The quiet ones were mostly those who wanted to stay loyal to Britain and King George.

After the noise died down, the Congress offered Paul some food. He ate and prepared to head back to Boston. Samuel Adams went over to talk with him, and I clung to his sleeve to get close enough to hear.

"This was a good thing you did, Paul," said Samuel. "I think the Resolves did just what I've been trying to do—stir the men to action."

Paul smiled. "I thought that it would. I came as quickly as I could make it."

"How long did it take you?" asked Samuel.

"A week's time," replied Paul.

"A week! Why, that's a ten day's ride for any man. How did you make it so fast?"

"The urgency of the matter pushed me on. I think I'll take things a bit slower heading home." Both men laughed.

Seven days! That had to be some kind of record. I liked this Paul Revere man. He seemed to be less interested in talking. He was a man of action.

As Paul rose from his seat to leave, I knew that I had to do something. The thought of spending any more time in Carpenter's Hall was too much. I had to go with Paul Revere. If there was adventure to be had, I knew this man would find it.

As Paul prepared to leave, he shook Samuel's hand. Then, luckily for me, he brushed Samuel's arm as he walked out of the building, and I grabbed on! I didn't think he noticed me, thankfully. When he climbed onto his horse, I dropped into his saddlebag. I figured this was a safe place to be. I didn't want to risk being separated from Paul. I could also see what was going on through a small hole in the side of the bag.

It would be weeks before we received word about what the Congress had decided. They, too, had adopted the Suffolk Resolves. This showed that they agreed with the men of Suffolk County and would take similar action in their own colonies.

The First Continental Congress also organized a boycott. No one in the colonies was to purchase anything made in Britian. This was the best way to punish the King for the Intolerable Acts. They hoped British merchants, who would lose money from the boycott, would pressure the King to reverse the acts. The British government would also lose money by not being able to collect the taxes on imported goods.

I was glad to hear the Congress had made some decisions. However, I was also glad that I hadn't stayed with them. Traveling with Paul Revere was a nice change of pace. I had a feeling, though, that things were going to get a lot more interesting.

Paul Revere was not just a messenger. In fact, a lot of his time was spent working at his day job. When I first arrived at Paul's shop as he carried me in his saddlebag, I wasn't sure what kind of work he did. There were some clues to help me figure it out though. Paul's shop had many tools hanging on the walls. There were hammers of all shapes and sizes. I also noticed several large anvils, and a huge fireplace was on one side of the room.

There were other things in the shop as well. There in the corner was a basket with old shoe buckles and bent spoons. There were also several lovely silver tea pots and bowls.

Hmm…what did Paul Revere do? I didn't think that he owned a tea shop. In fact, after the Boston Tea Party, I would have bet that he did not serve tea to anyone. Perhaps he was a cobbler. (A cobbler is someone who makes or repairs shoes.) A cobbler would have all those broken shoe buckles. The only problem with that idea was that there were no shoes in Paul Revere's shop.

It was early the next morning when someone came into the empty shop. I hoped it was Paul as I was eager to see just what it was that he did for a

living. I was surprised to find that instead of Paul, it was his son. He quickly got to work building up a fire in the fireplace.

Boy, was it hot! I guess I shouldn't have whined back when I was with the Congress. It had been pretty hot then. In Paul's shop now with the fire blazing, it was really hot. I evaporated in no time. I floated towards a shelf as far from the fire as I could get. It was cooler in the darkness of the shelf, and I quickly condensed onto a piece of metal. I had a good view of the room from there. I was looking forward to watching the two Reveres get to work.

Paul Jr. was just a teenager. Even still, he seemed confident working in the shop. He must have worked there a lot. When his dad came into the shop, he asked him about the trip to Philadelphia. As he talked, he headed right towards the shelf I was on. Had he spotted me?

He grabbed the metal I was on and threw it into a pot. I held on as tightly as I could. Where was I going next? It was hard to tell since I couldn't see out of the pot.

The pot stopped moving. A lid was put on top. I still couldn't see anything. I could hear the crackling of the fire. It seemed close, almost too close.

Was it just me or was it getting hot in here? I mean really, really hot. I noticed that the metal was starting to melt. I had never seen melted metal before. I thought I might get a closer look, but no such luck. It was just too hot. I was now a vapor.

There was only one little problem. I couldn't get out! The lid kept me in the pot. There was no escape as the temperature continued to rise.

Of course, since I am a water molecule I don't get hurt by such high heat. Isn't that a good thing? I still didn't like being stuck in anything—especially that pot!

In a few minutes, I felt the pot move as it was taken from the fire. Paul Jr. lifted the lid, and I quite literally blasted out of the pot and slammed into the ceiling. I sure was glad to be out of there!

"Be careful with that silver, son," said the older Revere.

"Don't worry, Father, I'm always careful. Silver that's been melted to two thousand degrees certainly isn't something to mess with."

Two thousand degrees! No wonder I had been so hot. The silver was poured into a cast iron mold and left to cool. Once the silver was molded, Paul Sr. took it out of the mold and began to shape it with his hammer on the anvil. Clang! Clang! Clang! The hammering was so loud that it rattled the windows.

Slowly, the piece of silver began to take shape. From time to time he would place the silver back into the fire, then quickly plunge it into a tub of water to cool. "You've got to keep the silver soft," he said to Paul Jr.

Finally, after what seemed like forever, he held up a bowl. "I think that will do," he said. I was surprised. Sure, it looked like a bowl. It just wasn't a very pretty one. It didn't look shiny like the other pieces of silver in the shop.

"Give it a good polish, my boy. All that heating up and cooling down sure does give it a tarnish." Paul Jr. took the bowl and began rubbing it down.

The entry doorbell sounded as a man entered the room. I did not recognize him. "Hello, Paul," he said. "Can I speak with you privately for a moment?"

"Of course," said Paul. His son left the room.

"How was Philadelphia?" The man asked.

"A grueling trip, but worth it, I think. The Congress needed to hear what the men of Suffolk County had to say. Has anything transpired in my absence?"

"Nothing of note," replied the man.

"Very good then," said Paul. "I will return to my post now that I am back. I will keep watch for any sudden movements of the army."

"And I as well," said the man.

"I will alert the other Committees when needed," Paul said.

Revere was referring to the Committees of Correspondence. I had heard talk about these at different times. They were groups organized by the major cities in the colonies. Each group watched the actions of the British troops. If they did anything out of line, the committee would inform the other cities about what had happened. It was the only way the colonies could know what was going on.

The Committee of Correspondence in Boston employed Paul to take their news to the other cities. They used him because he was reliable, fast, and loyal to the cause. Because of his post, Revere was often one of the first to know what was going on. He also aided the cause by spying on the British troops.

It was a long winter. Paul Revere stayed very busy, but not with his regular job. He was always taking a message or out watching the troops. He was so busy, in fact, that he had little time for smithing silver. Paul Jr. ended up running the shop while his dad was away.

The cold winter left me frozen to Paul's overcoat much of the time, so I often tagged along while he ran errands or went home at night to be with his wife and children. Sometimes, I managed to warm up enough to stay in the shop with Paul Jr. I was just waiting for something to happen.

It seemed like all of Boston was waiting as well. The town militia continued to train and stockpile weapons and gunpowder. Paul knew that other cities were doing the same. Everyone was preparing. When Spring came, something was going to happen. I just didn't know what.

Chapter Eight
A MIDNIGHT RIDE

It was mid-April when something finally did happen. The British army had gotten wind that the colonists were hiding weapons in the city of Concord. The plan was to find and destroy the supplies. I had heard Paul talk this over with his buddies. They knew the British would come. The only question was when and how.

It was a Tuesday evening, and Paul and his family were gathered around the dinner table. There was a swift knock at the door. Paul's wife answered it and told him, "A Dr. Joseph Warren to see you."

Paul rose from the table and headed toward the door. From my spot on his top collar button, I went with him. "Dr. Warren, what news do you bring?"

Dr. Warren spoke with a trembling voice. "The troops are mobilizing, sir. They are not in their normal posts. We fear they are headed out to arrest the good men Adams and Hancock, then on to Concord for the supplies."

One of Paul's little girls ran up to him and tugged on his pant leg. "Oh, Daddy, do come back inside. Your supper is getting cold!"

"Get back inside, child. This is not the time." She let out a whimper and ran back into the house.

I had never seen Paul speak to his children that way. "What task are you giving to me, Doctor?"

"Go to Reverend Clark's, where Adams and Hancock are staying. I have already sent Dawes ahead to alert them. Be sure they have received the message. Go on to Concord and tell the militia that the regulars are coming."

"Yes, sir," replied Paul.

"You won't be able to tell if the troops are coming by land or by sea—"

"Yes, I will. We made a plan last week in case this were to happen. One of my men will hang lanterns in the Old North Church steeple. One if the troops come by land, two if they are coming by sea."

"Why, that's genius," said Dr. Warren. "One if by land, two if by sea. Then if you are caught, the Sons of Liberty in Charlestown will still be able to spread the news."

"Plan for the worst; hope for the best. That's what I say. I had best get going," said Paul.

The two men shook hands. "Godspeed, my friend," said Dr. Warren.

I felt a rush of excitement. An adventure! Paul returned to the house and changed into his riding clothes. He kissed his wife and each of his children. "Take care of them, son," he said to Paul Jr. "If I am caught, it might be some time before I can return to Boston."

With that, we were out the door and into the street. Paul quickly headed to the north side of town where he met two men. They made no small talk. There was no time.

All three got into a small boat and rowed across the water. The moon was rising in the sky. The

men were silent as they crossed the water, watching with careful eyes.

We reached the shore, close to Charlestown. More men waited for us there. "We have seen several mounted troops," one of them said. "Something is surely afoot."

"I'll be needing a horse," Paul said.

A man stepped forward with a lovely mare. "Deacon Larkin has been kind enough to loan you his horse. She's fast and surefooted."

"That will do," said Paul. "Did you see the signals, then?"

"Yes, we did. Two lanterns. The regulars are coming by sea."

"Alright, then," said Paul. "I'm off to spread the warning. "We mounted the horse and rode off at a fast gallop. The men were right, the horse was fast. I held on to Paul's coat. It was a cool night, and the wind whipped about us.

It wasn't long before Paul stopped at a house and banged on the door. A man, still fully dressed despite the time of night, answered the door.

"Captain," said Paul. "The troops are coming by sea. They plan to capture Adams and Hancock and then take Concord. Ready your militia."

"Aye, Paul," said the captain.

In a flash, we were out the door and back at a full gallop. As we went along, Paul stopped at certain houses and shouted, "The regulars are coming out!" By the regulars, of course, he meant the British army. At house after house, it was like that. As we went along, it seemed like we were traveling faster and faster. I looked behind us and saw people coming out of their homes.

"The regulars are coming out!" shouted Paul again and again. I felt that I was a part of something important. If we did not alert the colonists, who would? There was no other way to communicate except person to person.

Paul Revere was determined to get the news out. When he arrived at the home of Reverend Clark, he wasted no time. He told Sam Adams and John Hancock what was going on. He took a brief rest to eat and was then back out the door and on his horse. There were more people to alert.

I listened to the horse's hooves pound into the earth. Suddenly the horse slowed her gait. Had she heard something? Wait! Over there! I thought I saw a flash of red in the moonlight. The horse must have seen it too, as she slid to a stop. We were surrounded by four redcoats on horses. We had been caught! What would happen now? There was no way to be sure, so I just kept quiet. Would anyone notice if I slowly slipped away?

"Your name, sir, and state your business," said one of the officers.

I hoped he wouldn't tell them the truth. It was the only safe thing to do. He must not have thought so. "I am Paul Revere, a silversmith from Boston. I ride to deliver news of the troop movements to the colonists."

The officers said some ugly things that I won't repeat here. "You'll have to come with us."

They searched him for weapons, and then we were on our way. I wondered what would happen to us. Paul Revere was a traitor, after all. He had betrayed King George and the British army. It's times like these that I'm glad to be a water molecule. I can't really choose a side, after all. All I can do is watch and see what happens.

We had ridden for a little ways when one of the officers came back and said to Paul, "We'll be taking your horse. You'll have to fend for yourself."

"I think we should just shoot him," said one of the other officers.

"He's not worth our time. Besides, we have to get moving, or we'll miss all the action."

The men took the horse and rode away. Paul and I stood under the moonlight. What would happen to us now?

Chapter Nine
LEXINGTON AND CONCORD

We walked along the roadside. In the distance, we heard the rat-a-tat-tat of the army drummers. Guns fired and men shouted in the distance. Paul and I both stayed quiet. A horse approached. It galloped straight toward us at full speed. The horse and rider passed us up, stopped a few yards past, and then turned back.

Paul stayed still as the rider approached. It was hard to see his face in the moonlight. "Who goes there?" the man asked. Oh no! I hoped that we weren't in trouble again. We had just gotten away from the British, and I didn't want to be captured again.

"Paul Revere," answered Paul. This man was always honest, wasn't he?

The horse neighed. "Of Boston?" asked the man.

"Yes, sir," said Paul.

"How did you end up here and without a horse, good fellow? I am Isaac Bissel."

"Isaac Bissell? The runner for the Lexington Committee of Correspondence?" Paul must have known him.

"One and the same," answered Isaac.

Paul seemed relieved. He told Isaac what had happened to us. "I was spreading the word that the army was coming, but I was soon overtaken by some regulars. They took my horse and left me alone. It is of no matter now. What news have you?" Why didn't Paul mention me? I had been there all along, after all. I guess it didn't matter.

"The war has begun!" Isaac answered with a bit of a shout.

Paul sighed. "I could tell that by the gunfire. How did it happen?"

Isaac answered, "The army came to destroy our weapons at Concord, but it was too late. Someone had already warned the militia that the British were coming. We moved the stockpile so it wouldn't be found."

Paul smiled. All of his riding was not in vain. He had alerted the troops in time. If he hadn't told them, the British might have found the weapons. The militia could never win a war without weapons!

Would Paul be famous one day? Would I? I could see the newspapers now: "Man and Molecule Ride to Save the Day!" Would they put the name Munford right there in print? Or would they leave it out to protect my identity?

Isaac continued his story. "The militia tried to stop the army from advancing. The regulars ordered them to put their weapons down."

"Who fired the first shot?" Paul wanted to know.

Isaac shook his head. "I'm not sure who. It all happened so fast. All I know is that many are wounded and some are dead."

Paul hung his head in sadness. "Where are you headed with the news?" he asked as he looked up.

"To Watertown," said Isaac. Hold on! Watertown? I had never heard of it. I wanted to go there. It really seemed like my kind of place. Maybe it was a whole town of water molecules. I had to know what it was like.

"Godspeed," said Paul.

"And the same to you," said Isaac. Paul smacked Isaac's horse on the rump. When he did,

I slid onto the horse and towards the saddle. I was going to Watertown.

We rode at full speed. It was much like the ride with Paul, except the sun was now up, making it easier to see. As we rode, the drumming became quieter and quieter.

The town was almost eight miles away, but it wasn't long before we were there. I noticed a few businesses with the name "Watertown" in them.

Isaac knew just where he was going. He must have been here before. This was clearly not the first message he had delivered here.

He jumped off of his horse and pulled a letter from his leather satchel. He knocked on the door of a house with a very loud thump thump thump.

A man answered the door. Isaac wasted no time. "Joseph Palmer, I have word from Lexington."

Mr. Palmer straightened up. "What is it?"

Isaac handed him the letter. Mr. Palmer read the letter with a trembling hand. When he was done, he quietly folded it up. "So, then...it has begun."

He sighed. "Who fired the first shot?" This was getting to be a common question.

Isaac frowned. "I do not know. Neither side was ordered to fire. I heard the militia captain, Parker, tell his men, 'Stand your ground; don't fire unless fired upon, but if they mean to have war, let it begin here.' That is all I know," said Isaac.

"I suppose it is of no matter," said Palmer. "Blood has been shed at the hands of the regulars. That is what counts. I'll have to draft you a note to carry to the next city." As Isaac stepped into the house, I dropped to the ground. I wanted to explore Watertown, after all.

The city was something of a let down. Watertown looked just like any other town. Of course, there were water molecules—we are everywhere, you know. Even so, it wasn't a city of all water molecules as I had wanted. It was sad, but I still held out hope. One day I'll find a place like that. Maybe I'll call it Watertown, too. Even better, I might call it Munfordville. That sounds good.

Isaac came out of the house a while later. He mounted his horse, and I knew he was headed to the next town to carry the message. I tried to catch him before he left, but I didn't make it.

I was stranded in Watertown. I sat down on a rock and wondered what I was going to do now. I wished that I had stayed with Paul Revere, but if I had I would have always wondered about Watertown. At least I would have been with the action if I had stayed with him.

The sun was now high in the sky and it slowly heated me up until I became a vapor. I floated up towards the sky, wondering where I would end up next.

Chapter Ten

THOMAS JEFFERSON

It was several weeks before I managed to find myself back on land. Wind and weather had carried me far. Too far, I thought. I had every reason to believe I was lost. I often wish that I could travel with a map because it would make life so much easier. Alas, I have never seen a map small enough for me to carry. Would it be strange to see a molecule of water carrying a map around? I think so!

I like maps. They help you know where you are going. Of course, they don't always have all the information you need, and sometimes you have to add things. I have been with explorers who did this. Often they started with a nearly blank map and filled it in as they went along. But enough about maps. Let's get back to my adventure. The last leg of my trip included a ride on a bird's beak. (I'm not sure what kind of bird.) It was quite a rush. I liked hearing the flapping of the bird's wings as we flew.

Traveling by bird is not like traveling by cloud. For one thing, clouds can get a little crowded, especially towards the end of a trip. Also, clouds don't take breaks. A bird has to stop every now and then to rest his wings. Oh, and he has to eat, of course.

All that stopping helped me to see a lot of cool stuff. One day, we might stop in a new city and the next might find us in a country orchard. Once, we took cover for the night in a horse stable.

Another day found us in a vegetable garden. It was quite pretty for a garden, and it had all kinds of vegetables. Some of them I did not recognize. Most were still young and tender, as it was not yet May. The bird must have thought it was quite a feast, for sure. He leaned in towards a piece of lettuce. I slid off of his wing and onto the plant. Just as he opened his beak, a woman began to shout. "Shoo! Shoo! Get out of here! Go on, bird!"

The bird flew away, flapping his wings as fast as they could go. Wait, bird! Don't forget me!

Oh, it was too late. The bird was gone, and I was left alone on the lettuce.

The bird-chaser woman carried a large woven basket filled with a mix of veggies from the garden. She walked up to the head of lettuce and plucked it right out of the ground. Of course, I had to go along, right into the basket. As the sun rose higher in the sky, we left the garden and headed towards a large brick house. It was very stately, more of a mansion than a house. It was not quite finished, and I saw some men laying brick on one side.

Inside, the kitchen was done, and several women worked to prepare dinner. I listened to them talk as they broke the beans. It seemed to me that they snapped the beans in a kind of rhythm as they worked.

They had just received news that a war had begun. It was the main thing they talked about.

"I reckon Mr. Jefferson will be going away again," said one of the ladies.

"Yes, I'm sure he will. Monticello won't be the same without him."

"No, it won't."

"Maybe this big ol' house will finally be done by the time he gets back."

"If it is, he'll just add something else to it. He loves this house too much to quit working on it."

Both of the women laughed. "There ain't many things he loves more than being home with his new wife."

The other woman nodded her head. "True, true. He does love Virginia colony, though. Why, defending the colonies is about the only thing that would make him leave home."

"You're right about that. We better get him his dinner so he can be on his way."

I ended up on a dinner plate right on top of a big mound of mashed potatoes. I swam in the pool of gravy and hoped I would get to meet the man of the house, although I really didn't want to be eaten by him. A human's stomach isn't any better than a cat's.

The ladies put the plate on a tray with several other things, then carried that whole tray and put it on a shelf. Can you believe it? It didn't make any sense. Were they just going to leave the food there until it got cold? I thought those old ladies had lost their minds.

Squeak! What was that? The tray started to rattle. What was going on? Was it an earthquake? I thought that I could almost hear the turning of gears, and it kind of felt like the tray was moving. Yes, it was. Squuuuueeak! Eek! The shelves spun around.

I was now in an entirely different room. The shelves must have been attached to some kind of revolving door. I was now in the dining room. A man came over and took the plate right off the tray and placed it at the head of the table. I looked up to see who might be consuming me. It was a tall, thin man who appeared to be in his mid-thirties. His wispy red hair offset his pointed nose.

He had been reading a book but set it down on the table now that his food had arrived. I wondered how long it would be before he ate me! The dining room was very large. It was also very fancy. Well, I guess if one is going to be eaten, at least it should be in a nice place like this one.

"I'm so sorry I must cut our visit short," said the red haired man.

"As am I, Mr. Jefferson," said another man at the table. "I understand that duty calls."

Jefferson sighed. "The Congress has been reconvened. There are many important decisions to be made. War changes much." He picked at the food on his plate with a fork, then took a bite of his beans. I was glad he had not yet gotten to his potatoes.

"It is a comfort," said the dinner guest, "that men like you will be representing Virginia. I know you will look out for our best interests."

"For Viriginia and all of the colonies, I hope. The King can no longer hold us in bondage."

"Hear! Hear! Do be careful, though. You'll be voting on things that the King has given you no power over. It's treason, you know."

"Only if we lose the war," said Jefferson. "Still, it is enough to make a man lose his appetite. I think I've eaten enough." He pushed his plate back. Yes! I had managed to escape being his dinner.

The guest also set down his fork. "I wish you safe travel and wisdom to know what is right."

"Thank you," said Jefferson. "I'll need it."

Chapter Eleven
SECOND CONTINENTAL CONGRESS

The plate was carried back to the kitchen by one of the staff. I was, of course, taken with it. I hoped I would be able to get back to Mr. Jefferson before he left for Philadelphia! I fell off of the plate and onto the kitchen counter as the ladies were cleaning up the supper mess.

Early the next morning, the cook rose and came into the kitchen. She was packing up a picnic basket for Mr. Jefferson to take on his way to Philadelphia. I knew I had to get into that basket! The only question was how...

The cook took out a loaf of fresh bread and set it down next to me on the table. It was still steaming from the oven. It put off so much heat that I soon found myself vaporized and floating through the air. I slammed into the side of the picnic basket lid. It was much cooler now away from the bread, and I condensed back into liquid form. Yes! I had made it into the basket and could now be sure I would get to go with Mr. Jefferson.

The ride to Philadelphia was much like the one I had taken some time ago with Samuel Adams. Thomas seemed to handle it a bit better, but he was of course much younger than Samuel Adams. In fact, he was only thirty-three years old.

While Samuel had been content to quietly think during the ride, Thomas was not. He ate a quick snack from his basket, wiping his mouth with the rag I had ended up on. I fell onto his shirt collar, thankful to be out of the basket and now able to see what was going on. Mr. Jefferson had a large stack of letters that needed to be answered so he pulled out his paper, ink well, and quill pen. How was he ever going to write in the back of a carriage? He tried placing his paper next to him on the seat, balancing the ink well in one hand and his quill pen in the other.

I watched from his shoulder as he hunched down and tried to write. I could hardly read what the paper said. His writing seemed to follow the bumps in the seat cushion.

"Well, that isn't going to work," he said as he stretched out what he had just written.

Still, he wasn't going to give up. He next placed the paper on his lap. "Much better," he said. But just as he started writing, the carriage hit a pothole in the road. Splash! Black ink spilled over the edge of the

ink well, it covered his paper, and seeped onto his trousers. "That's it! I'll never get my letters written at this rate." So, it was back to thinking for Mr. Jefferson. No more writing.

We arrived in Philadelphia one sunny afternoon. I could tell that Mr. Jefferson was anxious to get to work. Imagine my surprise when he shouted to the carriage driver, "STOP!"

"Whoa, there," said the driver as he pulled at the horse's reins.

"Thank you," said Mr. Jefferson. "I'll only be a few moments."

He climbed out of the carriage and walked up the steps and into a building. "B. Randolph, Cabinet Maker," read the sign.

I waited in the carriage until he returned a few moments later. What had he done? He told the driver to head on to their next stop, but he gave no clues about what he had done at the cabinetmaker. Strange.

On May 10th, Congress met at the Pennsylvania State House. It was the new location of the Congress. There were quite a few new men in Congress this time around. There were also many from the First Congress. Samuel Adams was there as was his friend John Hancock.

The men got right down to business. Something had to be done about the war. Some of the delegates, Sam Adams among them, wanted to break all ties with Britain. It seemed unlikely to them that Britain and the colonies would ever make up. Many of the delegates thought it was too early to claim independence. They thought the war would have to get worse before the colonists would go for such a daring move.

Since no one seemed to agree on this subject, it was on to other business. The colonies needed an army, and fast. Many cities had their own militias, but each was a small force, not capable of much damage. They must be combined into one army to provide the best defense for the colonies.

This new army would need a leader. The delegates debated, as usual, and then cast a vote. They chose a man named George Washington. This man was now the commander of the colonial army.

He had quite a job to do, that's for sure. The army wasn't even really an army. It was just a collection of undertrained militias and new soldiers. What was he going to do? Mr. Washington left Congress almost as soon as the vote was made. There was no time to be wasted. He had to get his army in order.

I won't go into the boring details about where I've been all this time. There was a trip to the laundry while on Mr. Jefferson's collar... Then there was an unfortunate incident with a flea and a field mouse... It is all very uninteresting when compared with what was going on in Congress.

I found myself a little while later in an overflowing rain cloud. As I headed towards the earth in a raindrop with some other molecules, the wind blew us sideways and through the open window of a building.

"Close that window!" someone shouted. "Don't let the wood get wet!"

A young boy frantically tugged at the open window until it shut with a thud. An older gentleman came and wiped at the wood that I was on. He managed to get most of the water off, but I was left behind in the woodwork.

After being there a few days, I realized that I was in a cabinet shop. There were lots of comings and goings, but I still stayed in the same spot. I wondered if Mr. Jefferson noticed that I was no longer traveling with him. I sure was starting to get lonely.

One day I heard the front door jingle as a new customer entered. Imagine my surprise when I heard the owner's voice calling out a name most familiar to me. "Mr. Jefferson! I am so glad to see you. Let me just go to the back and I'll get it." In a few moments, the wood I was on was being lifted up and carried to the front of the store.

There at the counter stood Thomas Jefferson himself. His eyes lit up when he saw me. He must have missed me after all! "Wonderful!" he said.

"I'm so glad you like it," said the cabinetmaker. He handed Mr. Jefferson a key.

Thomas ran his hands over the smooth, shiny wood, wiping me onto his finger. Boy! It was so nice

to be off of that wood. He inserted the key into a small lock and turned. Click! He opened up a small drawer on the side. It had dividers, but for what? He closed the drawer and lifted the lid. It did not open to the inside of the box. It merely folded back on a set of hinges.

"Magnificent, Benjamin. This is exactly what I wanted." He folded the lid down and tucked the key in his coat pocket.

"I followed your instructions to the letter," said Benjamin the cabinetmaker.

Thomas paid the man and carried the box out by its handle. Once in the carriage, he opened the side drawer back up. He neatly filled it with his paper, several ink wells, and pens. "Ah, it's perfect," he said. "If I do say so myself."

I still wasn't sure what was so great about the box, but it didn't matter to me. I was back with Mr. Jefferson. As the carriage pulled away towards the State House, Thomas took out a sheet of paper. He placed the paper on the top of the box. His ink well fit perfectly in one corner. He took out his pen and began to write. Genius! Now he could write wherever he was. No more spilled ink, to be sure.

Chapter Twelve

THOMAS PAINE

Congress convened for months. There was lots of debate, as usual. Mr. Jefferson didn't say as much as some of the other delegates. He did keep writing, however. That little desk of his was open at his bedside late into most nights.

News from the warfront came often. Sometimes it was news of a colonial victory, but often it was news of defeat. Almost always the news came with a request for more funds. The army needed clothes, weapons, ammunition, and food. The soldiers expected payment for their work.

There was one tiny problem. The Congress was still new and didn't have any funds saved up like Britain did. It also had no authority to tax the people. Only King George could do that. How could they send money when they had none? How could they get money if they couldn't collect taxes? The Congress had to ask the colonies for money. Each delegate put pressure on his colony to donate to the cause. Sometimes it worked, sometimes it didn't.

To make matters worse, not all of the colonists supported the war. Some just wanted to go back to the way things were. They would be more than willing to pay a tax on tea or anything else if they didn't have

to fight in the war. Things weren't going as well as could be hoped. Something needed to change in the minds of the people. If everyone supported the war and the Congress, more could be done. Victory would be closer.

Then things started changing. Congress received news that something called *Common Sense* had stirred many of the colonists to action against Britain. I overheard Samuel Adams talking with another delegate on the subject.

"What is it that has caused all this uproar?" asked Samuel.

"Why," said one of the delegates, "it is nothing more than a pamphlet, not even fifty pages long."

"It must be an impressive fifty pages. It seems that everyone is talking about it," said Samuel. "What does it say?"

"Well, all the same things we've been saying, really. That the King has not been treating us well. Also, it says that Britain is too far away to rule the Americas. It says men should be ruled by the law, not by a king."

Samuel leaned back in his chair. "It sounds like the author squeezed quite a bit into so few pages. Perhaps he thought no one would read it if it were any longer."

"Precisely. He also wrote it in plain language. Even the most common man can understand what he has to say."

"Smart man. Who did you say wrote it?" Samuel asked.

"Well, it was published anonymously. I think the writer did not want to be hung at the gallows. What he writes is treason to King George."

Thomas Jefferson walked over to the two men. "I couldn't help but overhear you talking about *Common Sense*. I've read it myself. Quite good stuff, I must say."

"Do you know who wrote it?" asked Samuel.

"Actually, I do. It was Thomas Paine, a good friend of Benjamin Franklin's. His goal is that every man in the colonies read it."

"Well, I bet he'll be making a pretty penny off of that."

"Actually, he won't," said Mr. Jefferson. "He wants to support the war. He donates his royalties to Washington's army to help buy supplies for the soldiers."

"He must be a generous man. I do hope that everyone will read it—if it will change their minds."

"As do I," said Mr. Jefferson. "As do I."

Chapter Thirteen

DECLARATION OF INDEPENDENCE

Well, here's the thing about being a water molecule. Sometimes you just get stuck. It happens more than you might think. All it takes is one stagnant pond or one tightly sealed bottle. There isn't a thing you can do about it but sit, wait, and hope for the best.

You see, I'm pretty strong. No matter how strong I am, though, I still need a little something to help me along. (At least every now and then.) You've been with me long enough now to know how it works. The wind can blow me along, or the sun can help me change forms. I rely a lot on these things to help me.

There is something else that helps me move from time to time as well. Maybe you've heard of it; it is called gravity. Now, you can't see it with your eyes. You can't hear it with your ears. You can't even feel it. But even if you don't see it, gravity is really important. It is the force that pulls you towards the earth so you don't fall off. It is always pulling me down, too. Sometimes that is a good thing. Sometimes it isn't.

It happened one day when Thomas Jefferson was writing something at the State Hall. (I know, I know. He's always doing that.) I wasn't paying much attention. I was just lounging on his shirt sleeve. Well, he dipped his quill pen in the ink. Suddenly, I lost my balance and the next thing you know, I tumbled right into that ink. No kidding. Good old gravity had done its job on me. Now I was swimming in ooey, gooey black ink.

You know I'm not one to stay in one place. I like to travel around, see the sights. Imagine how bad it was when I ended up spending months inside that ink well. I thought I might escape when Congress wrote the Olive Branch Petition. (Mr. Jefferson wrote part of it, of course.) It was basically a document asking the King to make amends with the colonies. I guess they thought that old King George might sign that, and the war would be over.

Well, would you believe that those men signed that Petition out of the wrong ink well? I guess it didn't matter to them which one they used. It sure mattered to me, though. I thought maybe

the King would send something else back that the Congressmen would need to sign. Nope. He didn't pay any attention to the Petition. I guess he was too mad over all the fighting.

If peace could not be made, what should happen next? Some of the delegates thought that the colonies should declare freedom from Great Britian. As a matter of fact, more and more of the colonists felt that way, too. By now many of them had read things like Common Sense and better understood what was going on.

I listened from my spot in the ink well as the men debated about freedom. Both sides had their points, I thought. Still, I wished they would agree on something so I could get out of this ink well. I had been cooped up long enough!

They finally decided to take a vote, but not all of the delegates voted. Some of them had been told by the colonists back home that they weren't allowed to make a big decision like that. It was just too risky. The ones who could vote, did. They voted to be free from Britain and King George. Did they know what they were getting themselves into? They would be killed for sure if the army ever got hold of them now.

They also voted to form a committee. The committee's job was to write up a document telling the reasons that the colonies wanted freedom. All the colonists would need to know and so would King George.

I knew one thing for sure—I wanted to be on that committee. From the way I saw it, they had a pretty important job. Besides, you might be surprised to find that dear old Munford here has quite a way with words. And maybe, just maybe, I wouldn't have to stay in this ink anymore.

The men on the committee spent a lot of time talking it over. What should the document say? Why did they want freedom? What else did they want? Once they had talked it over, they chose one man to write down all their ideas. I was happy to see that they chose someone I knew. It was my red haired friend from Virginia. You remember him, don't you? His name was Thomas Jefferson. Personally, I thought they might have been better off choosing me to write it. Still, I guess Jefferson was the next best thing. He did love to write.

At least he took his work seriously. He spent a lot of time working on this freedom document. He must have been thankful to have that portable desk of his. It sure did come in handy now as he wrote draft after draft.

He read a lot, too. He read what some of the other colonists had written about freedom. He even re-read some things that he had written about it. He didn't want to write something new. He simply wanted to clearly write down what everyone was thinking.

I stayed right there with him while he wrote. I tried to yell a few ideas out to him, but I don't think he heard them. At least, he didn't use any of them. Oh well.

When it was done, Jefferson's work was called the "Declaration of Independence." The whole thing sounded a little scary to me. I knew King George wouldn't like it a bit. "When in the course of human events," it began. After that, it was all a little bit over my head. Maybe if I weren't dripping in ink I might have understood a little better.

There was one part that really stuck out: "All men are created equal." I thought this was a pretty neat idea. No one man is better than another; the colonists wanted all to be treated fairly. It sounded like a good idea to me.

Thomas kept that thing locked up in his little desk, and I was right there with it, too. I guess if anyone tried to take it, I could stop them. If only I wasn't stu—never mind. I'm sure you're sick of my whining.

The men of the Congress really liked the Declaration, too. Of course, they couldn't just say that. They had to talk about it. They changed some things. They took some things out. Still, the bulk of it was what Jefferson wrote.

Finally, on July 2nd, 1776 the men of the Congress voted to adopt the Declaration of Independence. The Declaration said, that they "... solemnly publish and declare, that these United Colonies are, and of right ought to be free and independent states; that they are absolved from all allegiance to the British crown, and that all political connection between them and the state of Great Britain, is and ought to be totally dissolved..."

It was quite a mouthful, but it made things very clear. The colonies would no longer be under British rule. They had now officially formed their own government. It was more important than ever that they win the war.

It was two whole days before Congress got around to signing the Declaration. They sure did take their time, didn't they? It was okay, though. One of the men from Boston, John Hancock, signed it first. He picked up the quill pen and his hand trembled a bit. He must have known how important this was. He reached over towards the inks...He dipped it into my ink well...I grabbed on!

As he signed his first name, I clung to the pen, then went with the ink. Right as he made the capital H on his last name, I went onto the paper. I was now a part of the Declaration of Independence! Mr. Hancock stepped back and

admired his work. He didn't seem to mind that
I was there. I was only right in the middle of his
name. You wouldn't mind, would you?

I was pretty proud of myself. I was right smack
dab on an historical document, after all. Then I had
a scary thought. Could I get in trouble? Would King
George hang me for treason? Being a water molecule,
I don't think he could punish me in that way. How
would he punish me, then? I bet he would think of

something. So I changed my mind. Sure, I was glad to be out of that ink well. I just didn't want to be where I was now. I might even go back to the ink well if it meant I would be safe from the King.

What were these men thinking? They were risking their lives to sign a silly piece of paper. I wasn't sure it was such a good idea. Why did they do it then?

All I can figure is that they really wanted to be free. They wanted a government that would treat them fairly. They wanted a government that would listen to their ideas. They wanted a government that they chose instead of a King who got the job by default.

Of course, signing a piece of paper didn't make it official. To truly be free from the King's grasp, the colonies would have to win the war. That would prove to be no easy task.

Chapter Twelve
VALLEY FORGE

The Declaration was kept rolled up and stored away most of the time. So even though I evaporated quickly from my place in the ink, I couldn't escape the roll of parchment. Lucky for me, I didn't stay with the Declaration forever. Okay, well, I did stay for a while. About a year, actually. By the time I got free from that thing, I was fit to be tied. I guess I understood why those colonists wanted freedom so badly.

It had been a year, but the men in Congress still had a lot of work to do. They had to find money to fight the war. They had to unite the thirteen separate colonies. They had to decide how this new government would work. All this meant one thing: talking. There was lots of it, as usual.

I was trying to decide what to do next when Congress received some bad news. The British soldiers were marching towards Philadelphia. They were going to try and take the city. If they did, all of Congress would be taken captive.

As soon as the men of Congress heard, they started packing up their things. They were able to leave the city just in the nick of time. It was a good thing, too, because in September the British took Philadelphia for their own.

I stayed with Congress as they set up their new meeting hall north of Philadelphia. One day a messenger arrived. Commander Washington had sent him, and he brought news from the war front. Congress drafted a message for Washington. I was glad when I got rubbed onto the message from someone's sweaty palm. I wanted to meet up with George Washington again. He was quite famous now and had won some important battles. Of course, he had lost some, too.

By the time I left Congress, summer was winding down. The leaves were turning to fall colors, and most of the crops were harvested. Everyone was preparing for winter. The army was preparing, too. Before long, it would be too cold for anyone to fight.

I arrived at Washington's camp in January of 1777. It was cold, really cold. Freezing cold. When he read the message from Congress, I fell onto his winter coat, where I ended up frozen solid. It was quite an honor to be on the jacket of such a great man.

Washington and his men had made their camp in Valley Forge, Pennsylvania. It was a good spot, safe from surprise attacks. Still, it wasn't so far that army scouts couldn't keep their eyes on things. There were over ten thousand men at Valley Forge. They lived in large bunkhouses that they had built themselves. Things were a little cramped.

There weren't just men there either; there were some women as well. Mostly they were the wives of the soldiers, and they helped with the cooking and the laundry. They even acted as nurses at times.

George Washington hated to see his men suffer. They had worked so hard. He did not want them to go without food, clothing, or a paycheck.

Still, there was little he could do as blankets of snow covered the landscape. The main problem was a lack of funds. Even with the recent changes, the Congress still did not have enough money to fund the war, which had gone on for so long now that it was starting to take a toll.

The weather didn't help things either. Sometimes snow fell so thickly that you couldn't see what was going on around you. (Don't blame the snow, though. We are just doing our jobs.) The men

had not had new clothes in many months. In some cases, their shoes had fallen apart on the long march to Valley Forge and had not yet been replaced. The cold, along with thin, ragged clothing, made many men sick.

The sickness spread through the camp like wildfire, and hundreds of men died. There weren't enough doctors to take care of everyone. There were not enough supplies, either.

Washington had picked this isolated spot for camp so the British could not attack. Sadly, it also made it difficult to get supplies into the camp. Food did come, but not always enough to feed all the men a hearty meal. I was glad I didn't have a stomach that needed filling.

I didn't get quite the adventure I was hoping for at camp, because it was a sad place to be. I did get to know Washington, though. He was a good man and a strong leader who did all he could to take care of his soldiers. I admired him for that. So did the men, I think. He tried to make the best of the bad times.

On February 23, a Prussian baron arrived at Valley Forge. His name was von Stuben, and he seemed like a strange young man to me. Washington was too busy to pay much attention to him. That is, until von Stuben showed him a letter he had brought along. Washington read it with great interest.

"So you know Benjamin Franklin, then?" he asked of the young baron.

"Yes, I do. He thought I could be of service to your cause. Whatever you need," he told Washington in his native tongue. He spoke very little English, but others were able to translate for him.

Washington seemed to like von Stuben and asked him to help drill the army. The General needed his ragtag militiamen turned into a disciplined army force.

Von Stuben was up to the task. He worked for the next few months drilling the men day in and day out. When he was done, they could follow the commands of their leaders. They stood taller and walked straighter. If it weren't for their mismatched uniforms, one might have mistaken them for the British army.

The men who managed to survive the winter were relieved when spring arrived. They were now a real army, ready to defeat and take down the British. They were well rested and exercised. The time had come for Victory.

The creek next to the camp was no longer frozen from winter's cold. It had melted and was now bubbling along. As one of the soldiers bent down to wash his face, he washed me into the creek along with the dirt from his face. I was swept down the

creek with millions of other molecules, and this was the end of my adventure with the fiesty colonists.

I had a feeling, though, that the colonists would triumph over the British. Their determination would see them through. With men like Samuel Adams and Thomas Jefferson and George Washington leading the way, I knew that the best was yet to come.

I was off to something new. Who knew what exciting thing I would do next? I hope you'll join me, whatever it might be.

...and the rest is history.

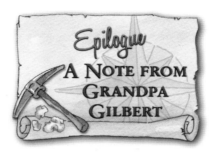

Epilogue

A NOTE FROM GRANDPA GILBERT

George Washington did lead the colonial army to Victory. The British surrendered to the colonists in October, 1781. General Washington went on to become the first President of the United States and has been fondly remembered as the "Father of his Country." He served two terms as president and coined the title "Mr. President," when others proposed using more majestic titles such as, "Your Most Excellent Highness."

Thomas Jefferson became famous all over the world for his work authoring the Declaration of Independence. He served as the first Secretary of State, was Vice President to John Adams, and later became the third President of the United States.

Samuel Adams became known as the "Father of the American Revolution" because of his firm stand against the tyranny of the British Crown. He served in the Continental Congress and was a signer of both the Articles of Confederation and the Declaration of Independence.

Paul Revere is still known for his skill as a silversmith. He helped provide supplies for the army during the Revolutionary War. He established gunpowder mills, built a furnace near Boston Harbor to make parts for American ships, and made cannons from iron and brass. He cast the first bell ever made in Boston, and many of his bells can still be found hanging in Boston today.

Thomas Paine's *Common Sense* was not only a success in the colonies but overseas as well. It was translated into German and printed in England, France, Holland, and Scotland. One hundred twenty thousand copies were sold during the first three months, and over six million copies have been sold since its first printing.

The thirteen American Colonies eventually grew to fifty states and is known the world over as the land of the free.

The American Revolution

FASCINATING FACTS

- The famous battle of Bunker Hill was actually fought on Breed's Hill.

- The first submarine ever used in battle was in New York Harbor in 1776 during the Revolutionary War. This sub, the *Turtle*, was supposed to attach a flintlock bomb to the hull of the *Eagle* and slip away before it detonated. Unfortunately, it failed in its mission when it got entangled in the *Eagle's* rudder bar.

- The French played an important role in the Colonists' successful battles with the British. They supplied nearly 90% of the gun powder used by the Colonists.

- George Washington did not accept pay for his service in the military.

- The population of the Colonies was 3,500,000.

- The Stamp Act, imposed upon the colonists by the British, required a tax to be paid on printed materials including newspapers, legal document, and other types of paper.

- Thomas Jefferson died on July 4, 1826, exactly 50 years after Declaration of Independence.

- John Adams represented the British soldiers at their trial for the Boston Massacre. This showed the world that in America everyone has the opportunity to defend themselves in a court of law.

The American Revolution

INTERESTING ACCOMPLISHMENTS

- Paul Revere is credited with developing rolled sheet copper in the U.S.

- The Constitution of the United States of America is the longest standing constitution in the world.

- Thomas Jefferson invented a number of useful items. One, the wheel cipher, was used to code messages. Another, was a revolving book stand that could fold into a box.

- George Washington is the only president to ever win 100% of the electoral votes.

- In May of 1775, Ethan Allen led the Green Mountain Boys and successfully took over the British garrison at Fort Ticonderoga without firing one shot.

- Benjamin Franklin represented Pennsylvania during the Second Continental Congress. He helped Jefferson with the Declaration of Independence. Among his many accomplishments he ran the first post office, founded the first hospital, established the first circulating library, created the lightning rod to prevent buildings from catching fire, invented bifocals and the Franklin stove.

SHARING THE VISION OF MUNFORD

I met Josh and Cindy Wiggers, the fine folks behind Geography Matters, while I was still in high school. Their kids and I went to church together and were becoming fast friends. It wasn't long before I went to the Wiggers house for a visit. Josh made quite an impression on me. First, he insisted that everyone call him Uncle Josh. Second, every conversation, it seemed, ended up turning into a geography drill. "What is the smallest country in the world? What is the capital of Zambia? What country is located between France and Spain?" Needless to say, all of these questions were a little overwhelming, but I kept going back for more visits and more geography drills.

Uncle Josh began telling me about a vision he had of a character he named Munford. He had first dreamed up the little water molecule many years before in a moment of inspiration while driving on the highway in the rain. Because Munford was water, he could be anywhere at anytime in history. By following his adventures, kids could learn about science, history, and geography. There would be almost no limit to what Munford could do. The only problem was that Uncle Josh hadn't been able to find a writer that was a good match for Munford. He had heard that writing was a hobby of mine, and wanted me to give it a try. I'm not sure exactly why he chose to take a chance on me. I was only a sophomore in high school! He must have liked my sample chapter, though, because he asked me to finish the book (*Munford Meets Lewis and Clark*) and then write others (*The Klondike Gold Rush, The American Revolution*, and more to come...).

It was 2002 when I first set pen to page and wrote Munford's first adventure. Since then, Uncle Josh and the rest of the Wiggers family became like a part of my extended family. Geography Matters has grown and flourished as one of the best homeschooling publishers on the market today. Munford himself has gone through many changes, thanks to multiple revisions, illlustrators, and improvements.

Munford, who is actually a water molecule, is often referred to and portrayed as a water drop. A water drop is actually made of many water molecules, so I took some artistic license by calling him a drop. It is easier to understand and visualize Munford as a drop rather than a teeny, tiny, molecule that cannot be seen with the naked eye.

My hope for Munford is that he will teach your children without them even realizing how much they are learning. Who knows, if they ever have the chance to meet Uncle Josh, or someone like him, perhaps they will be able to answer those pesky geography, history, or science questions with pride.

Munford's Other Adventures

THE KLONDIKE GOLD RUSH

In this adventure, Munford finds himself slap into the middle of the Klondike Gold Rush. He catches gold fever on this dangerous, yet thrilling, adventure. Meet some of the Gold Rush's most famous characters, like gold baron Alex McDonald or the tricky villain named Soapy Smith. Take a ride on the Whitehorse Rapids, and help Munford as he pans for gold. This is an adventure you won't soon forget!

MUNFORD MEETS LEWIS & CLARK

Join him on an epic adventure with Meriwether Lewis and William Clark, as they make their perilous journey in search of the Northwest Passage to the Pacific Ocean. Munford will inspire your children to learn more about the Corps of Discovery and the expedition that changed the face of America.

MORE TO COME . . .

Look for more adventures in this exciting series as Munford's journey through time and territory continues around the world.

Other Titles Published by Geography Matters

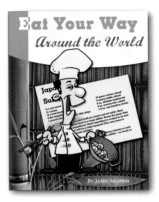

EAT YOUR WAY AROUND THE WORLD

by Jamie Aramini

Get out the sombrero for your Mexican fiesta! Chinese egg rolls… corn pancakes from Venezuela… fried plantains from Nigeria. All this, and more, is yours when you take your family on a whirlwind tour of over thirty countries in this unique international cookbook. Includes a full meal of recipes from each country. Recipes are easy to follow, and ingredients are readily available. Jam-packed with delicious dinners, divine drinks, and delectable desserts, this book is sure to please.

EAT YOUR WAY THROUGH THE USA

by Loreé Pettit

Taste your way around the U.S.A. without leaving your own dining room table! Each state has its unique geographical features, culinary specialities, and agricultural products. These influence both the ingredients that go into a recipe and the way food is prepared. Compliment your geography lesson and tantalize your tastebuds at the same time with this outstanding cookbook. This cookbook includes a full meal of easy to follow recipes from each state. Recipes are easy to follow. Though they aren't written at a child's level, it's easy to include your students in the preparation of these dishes. Cooking together provides life skills and is a source of bonding and pride. More than just a cookbook, it is a taste buds-on approach to geography.

Other Titles Published by Geography Matters

Cantering the Country by Loree´ Pettit and Dari Mullins

Galloping the Globe by Loree´ Pettit and Dari Mullins

Trail Guide to…Geography **series** by Cindy Wiggers

Geography Through Art by Sharon Jeffus and Jamie Aramini

Trail Guide to Learning **curriculum series** by Debbie Strayer & Linda Fowler

Uncle Josh's Outline Map Book by George Wiggers and Hannah Wiggers

Uncle Josh's Outline Map Collection CD-ROM

Lewis and Clark, Hands On by Sharon Jeffus

Profiles from History **series** by Ashley Wiggers

Laminated Maps

Laminated Outline Maps

Mark-It Timeline of History

Timeline Figures CD-ROMs

And much more . . .

Geography Matters®
Make Learning Fun

Contact us for our current catalog,
or log on to our website.
Wholesale accounts and affiliates welcome.

(800) 426-4650   www.geomatters.com

About the Author

Jamie Aramini is the author of *Eat Your Way Around the World*, *Geography Through Art* with Sharon Jeffus, and the *Adventures of Munford* series. She graduated co-valedictorian of her high school class and was a Kentucky Governor's Scholar. She is currently raising her two sons, a flock of chickens, and a miniature Schnauzer named Sophie. Her hobbies include organic gardening, cooking, and teaching writing at her local homeschool co-op. Visit www.jamiearamini.com to learn more about Jamie.

About the Illustrator

Emily Lefferts is a homeschool graduate from Sutton, Massachusetts. She is currently studying visual arts with a concentration in illustration at Gordon College. Her courses at Gordon have taken her to Italy where she spent a semester studying art. After graduation, she hopes to continue working as an illustrator. She lives at home with seven siblings, four dogs, and two very patient parents.